P9-DCH-847

the POLAR BEAR Wish

By Lori Evert

Photographs by Per Breiehagen

Random House  New York

Text copyright © 2018 by Lori Evert
Jacket and interior photographs copyright © 2018 by Per Breiehagen

All rights reserved. Published in the United States by Random House Children's Books,
a division of Penguin Random House LLC, New York.

Random House and the colophon are registered trademarks of Penguin Random House LLC.

Visit us on the Web! rhcbooks.com

Educators and librarians, for a variety of teaching tools, visit us at RHTeachersLibrarians.com

For additional information about this book, visit TheWishBooks.net.

Library of Congress Cataloging-in-Publication Data is available upon request.
ISBN 978-1-5247-6566-8 (trade) — ISBN 978-1-5247-6567-5 (lib. bdg.) — ISBN 978-1-5247-6568-2 (ebook)

MANUFACTURED IN CHINA
10 9 8 7 6 5 4 3 2
First Edition

FOR SUE, PAUL, AND BRIA SCHURKE—
YOUR KINDNESS, GENEROSITY, AND CARE FOR THE ENVIRONMENT
MAKE THE WORLD A BETTER PLACE.

Gratitude:

*Many, many thanks to everyone at Wintergreen Dogsled Lodge for sharing
your amazing dogs and beautiful wonderland with us.
We can't wait to return to your magical place in the woods. (dogsledding.com)
Thank you to Oliver Krawczyk for bringing Erik to life in such a magnificent way.
Special thanks to Jennifer Hedberg of Wintercraft for creating our spectacular ice castle.*

Digital Artists: Per Breiehagen and Brad Palm

Long, long ago, so high in the mountains and close to the stars that on clear nights you didn't need a lantern, lived an adventurous girl named Anja.

One winter's eve as Anja was tucking her dog, Birki, in for the night, she told him, "We can't go to the Christmas party tomorrow because Papa needs the horse for work. I wish we had a dogsled so you could take us there."

She told him all about what the party would be like: There would be special treats and games and dancing around a big, fancy tree. There would be lots of children and dogs and horses to play with. Her cousin Erik and his dog, Bria, would be there too.

They drifted off to sleep with wishful thoughts of the wonderful party.

The night went by in a wink. Anja was awakened by big, wet kisses and thumping tails.

*A*nd Erik!

"Surprise!" he said. "We're going to the party. I've packed everything we need for the trip, with food and blankets in case of emergencies.

"My mama packed a breakfast for us and apples for the pups," Erik said.

*A*fter they had eaten their cheese sandwiches and cookies, Anja hitched up Birki and they were off.

Foxes and lynx and a bright red cardinal greeted them as they traveled through the woods. A light snow began to fall.

When they were out of the woods, the snow started to come down so hard that it became a blanket of white in front of their eyes. They couldn't even see the dogs!

They stopped and talked about turning back . . .
but they didn't know which way to go. They were lost.

The dogs started howling,
and soon they heard wolves
howling too. The wolves
sounded very close.

$\mathcal{T}$hen it was silent. The children could see gray shapes coming toward them through the snow. Were they wolves?

They *were* wolves. One spoke.

"Don't be afraid," she said. "Your dogs called for our help. We can take you to a tent that is set up for travelers passing through."

Anja and Erik were relieved to find shelter. They gave
the wolves apples to thank them; then they fed the dogs,
unpacked their blankets and food, and climbed into the tent.

Just as they were falling asleep, they heard scratching at the door of the tent.

"I'm glad my papa reminded me to pack a lantern," whispered Erik as he carefully lit the lantern.

They pushed open the flap of the tent and could not believe what they found: a baby polar bear! He looked scared, so they invited him into the tent.

"*W*hat is your name?" Anja asked gently.

"Tiny," he answered. "I've lost my mama in the storm. Can you help me find her?"

They were sorry for him, but it was hard not to smile because he was so cute and his voice was so small and squeaky. Without a second thought, they promised to help him; then they all settled down to sleep.

When they woke up, the baby polar bear was gone!

The children got out of the tent and found Tiny sleeping in the snow near the dogs.

"I was too warm in that tent," he squeaked. "And I was hoping my mama might come by and find me."

Everyone was happy that the storm was over.
They quickly ate, packed up, and set out with Tiny
riding on their packs.

"Let's head west, toward the sea," said Anja. "Maybe we will find your mama there."

They came upon some pack ice, and as they struggled to push up and down its ridges, they saw a bear they thought was Tiny's mother. But he yelled, "It's a male bear—turn back!"

They started to turn the sled around, but the enormous bear soon caught up with them.

"Anja! It's me—your friend Jager!" he said.
"The cardinal told me you were lost."

Anja was happy to see her friend again. Jager
told them he knew someone who could help find
Tiny's mama.

They traveled over a glacier and through beautiful frozen fjords.

At sunset, they reached a shimmering ice castle guarded by a majestic white reindeer.

Jager spoke to the reindeer, who agreed to guide them to Tiny's mother. Then she invited them into her castle.

"Let's all have dinner and a good night's sleep," said the reindeer. "We will leave first thing in the morning."

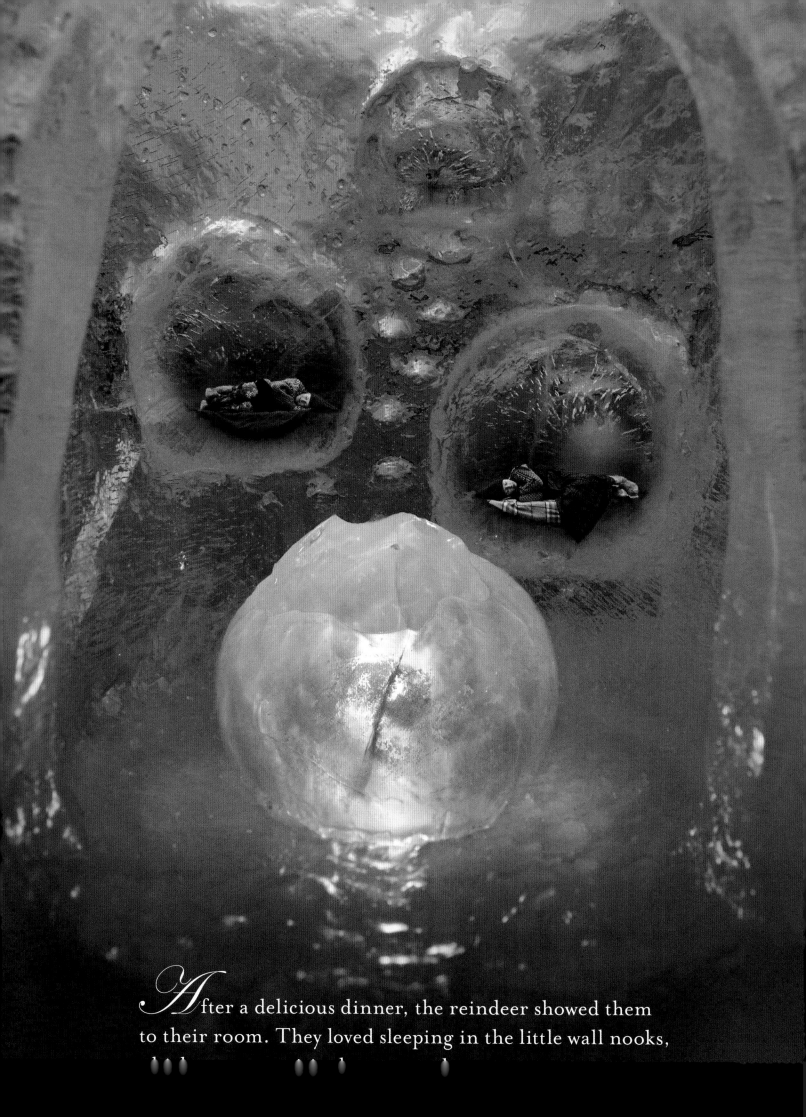

After a delicious dinner, the reindeer showed them
to their room. They loved sleeping in the little wall nooks,

The next morning, the reindeer led them up a steep mountainside. Anja and Erik pushed with all their strength, and Tiny hopped off the sled to help the dogs.

When they finally found Tiny's mama,
he ran to her and gave her a big hug and a kiss.

$\mathcal{T}$hen Tiny turned to his new friends and thanked them for their help.

"We'll miss you," Anja said. "But I'm happy you are home safe, and I hope we'll see each other soon."

*I*nstead of taking them home, the reindeer surprised them and took them to the Christmas party. It was just as Anja had imagined.

After much dancing, singing, nibbling, and laughing, they saw a cardinal alight on the top of the tree. He said, "It is time for everyone to go home and get their rest— tomorrow is Christmas Day!"

The reindeer led them to Erik's house first. After Anja helped him unpack, he pulled a ribbon off one of her braids and tied it to the sled.

"The sled is yours," he said. "Merry Christmas!"

Anja and Birki were thrilled. She thanked Erik and they said sleepy goodbyes. Anja rode home on the reindeer's back, and quickly fell asleep to the steady rhythm of his snowy walk.

Early Christmas morning, Anja was lying in bed thinking about her remarkable dream when she heard Birki barking. She looked out her window to see him hitched to a dogsled with a ribbon tied on it!

As she quickly pulled on her sweater and dress, she wondered if it *was* a dream, or if all that had happened was real.

*W*hat do you think?